It's extra exciting for Sarah and Ian.
They get to be the flower girl and ring bearer.
Ian is wearing a nice suit and Sarah got a new dress.

William and Aunt Olivia also look wonderful today.
William is wearing a top hat and Aunt Olivia is wearing
a beautiful wedding dress.
Ian and Sarah get to hold the veil.
They practiced a lot.
"Don't pull on the veil," Sarah says softly.
"No, and don't stick out your tongue or wave at the people,"
Ian whispers.

Very slowly,
they walk behind
the bride and groom.

What are Ian and Sarah wearing at the wedding?

What do Ian and Sarah eat at the wedding?

What do Ian and Sarah make?

What did Dad lose?

What do Ian and Sarah get to throw?

What do Ian and Sarah play with at the party?

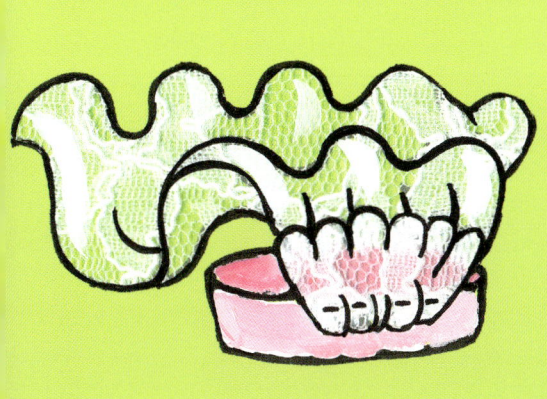

First published in Belgium and Holland by Clavis Uitgeverij, Hasselt – Amsterdam, 2015
Copyright © 2015, Clavis Uitgeverij

English translation from the Dutch by Clavis Publishing Inc. New York
Copyright © 2017 for the English language edition: Clavis Publishing Inc. New York

Visit us on the web at www.clavisbooks.com

No part of this publication may be reproduced or stored in a retrieval system,
or transmitted in any form or by any means, electronic, mechanical, photocopying,
recording, or otherwise, without the prior written permission of the publisher,
except in the case of brief quotations embodied in critical articles and reviews.
For information regarding permissions, write to Clavis Publishing, info-US@clavisbooks.com

Sarah at the Wedding written and illustrated by Pauline Oud
Original title: *Saar en het trouwfeest*
Translated from the Dutch by Clavis Publishing

ISBN 978-1-60537-331-7

This book was printed in February 2017 at Publikum d.o.o., Slavka Rodica 6, Belgrade, Serbia

First Edition
10 9 8 7 6 5 4 3 2 1

Clavis Publishing supports the First Amendment and celebrates the right to read

Sarah
at the Wedding

Pauline Oud

Clavis
NEW YORK

Today is a special day.
It's a party.
Not just a birthday party, but a really big party...
a wedding!
Aunt Olivia is getting married to William.

"We are gathered here today to celebrate the love between Olivia and William, who want to be together forever," says the man in front.
"William, do you want to marry Olivia?" the man asks.
"I do!" William says happily.
"Olivia, do you want to marry William?"
"I do," Aunt Olivia says.

"Now it's time for the rings!"
The man looks at Dad.
The rings are in the pocket of Dad's jacket. Or are they?
Dad looks in all his pockets. Where are the wedding rings?
Dad's face turns red. Did he lose the rings?
Are they still back home on the table?

"Found them!" Luckily the rings were in Dad's trouser pocket!
Dad quickly lays them on the little red pillow.
Ian and Sarah carry the rings to William and Aunt Olivia.

They walk very carefully.
Don't drop the pillow!
William puts a ring on Aunt Olivia's finger.
Then Aunt Olivia puts the other ring on William's.

"I now pronounce you... man and wife!"
Uncle William lifts his top hat and looks at Aunt Olivia with a sweet smile.
They kiss for a very long time.
Ian and Sarah think it's funny.
"Hooray!" Dad and Mom call.
"Hooray!" Grandpa calls.
Grandma is so happy she even cries a little.

There is a long red carpet outside.
A lot of people are waiting.
Ian and Sarah each have a basket filled with flowers.
They can throw the flowers in the air when Aunt Olivia and William come outside.
Everyone is clapping and they are all very happy.
Grandpa waves and does a little dance!

"Go and stand close together," the photographer says.
"Ian, look at me. Very good, Sarah, give me a nice smile!"
The photographer takes a lot of photos.
Ian and Sarah have to keep smiling.
It takes so long!
But then the photographer is finally done
and they go to the big party tent in the garden.

Sarah has never seen such a beautiful cake.
"It looks like three cakes!" Ian says.
There are two dolls on top of the cake.
They look exactly like William and Aunt Olivia!

William and Olivia cut the first pieces of the cake together.
"You don't like cake, do you?" William asks, laughing.
"Yes, I do!" Ian and Sarah answer at the same time.

Ian and Sarah's bellies are filled with cake.
They drink lemonade through a straw.
Then Grandpa has a surprise: bubbles!

"You first have to shake the bottle," Sarah says.
"Yes, and blow very gently!" Ian says happily.
While the other people talk and laugh in the garden, Ian and Sarah blow the biggest bubbles. Soon lots of beautiful bubbles are flying through the sky.

There is an arts and crafts table in the party tent. "Look, Grandma!" says Sarah when she sees pieces of white cloth. "It's just as pretty as Aunt Olivia's dress!" "Ha," Ian says, "I'll make a hat. Just like William's!"

"Shall we get married?" Sarah asks when they are done.
"Yes," Ian says. "Because you are my best friend."
Sarah takes two pieces of paper.
"Look, a ring for you and one for me."
"We are married!" Ian yells and he gives Sarah a big kiss!

The party goes on a long time.
There are French fries and there is
ice cream for the children.
When it gets dark, the little lamps
in the party tent go on. Pretty!
There is music and all the people are dancing.
Ian and Sarah cheerfully dance along.
They get to stay up very late tonight.
This wedding is so much fun!

Make your own veil...

What do you need?
A strip of heavy colored paper
A piece of nice cloth
A stapler

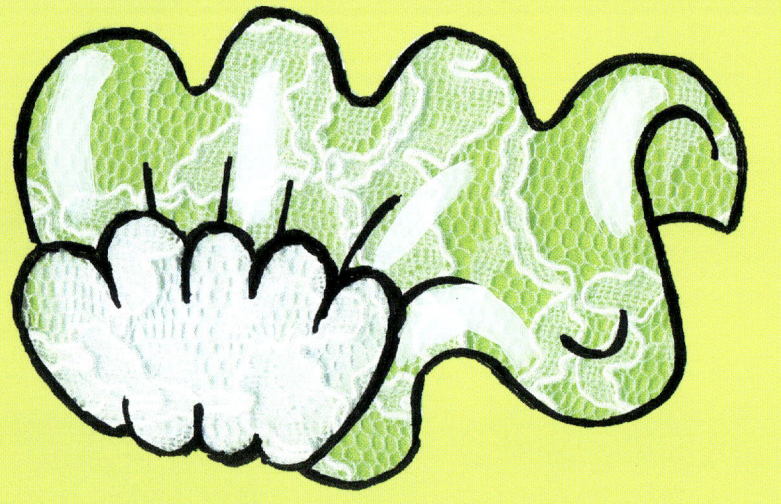

What do you do?
Staple the strip of colored paper in a circle.
Fold a piece of the cloth in half.
Fold pleats in it and staple it to the strip of paper.

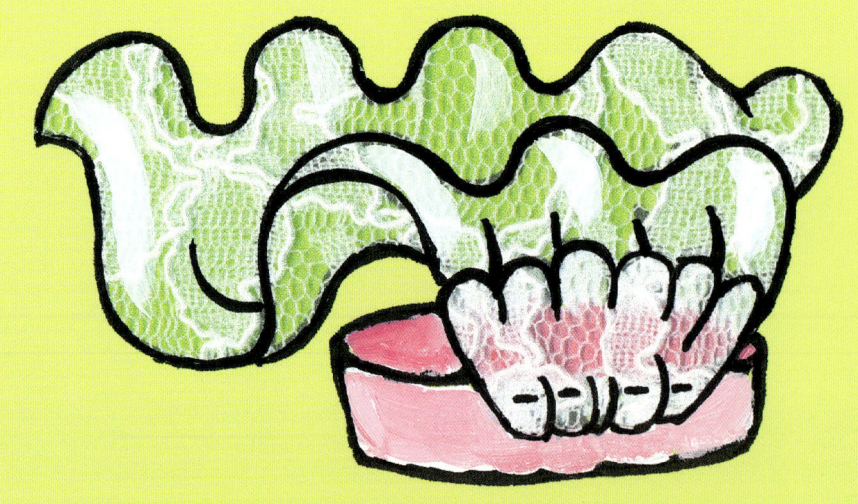

Your veil is ready!